Bear Takes a Trip
L'Ours fait un voyage

Stella Blackstone
Debbie Harter

Barefoot Books
step inside a story

7:00 am

Bear has a very long journey to make.
There are lots of things for him to take.

7h00

L'Ours a un très long voyage à faire.
Il a beaucoup de choses à emporter.

8:30 am

He makes his bed and washes his face.
He eats his breakfast and packs his case.

8h30

Il fait son lit et se lave le visage.
Il prend son petit déjeuner et fait sa valise.

9:00 am

He hops on the bus at the end of the lane.
It takes him through town where he'll get
on the train.

9h00

Il monte dans le bus au bout de la ruelle.
Il l'amène au centre-ville où il va prendre
le train.

10:00 am

He meets his friend, who is coming too.
They chat about everything they want to do.

10h00

Il rejoint son ami qui va l'accompagner.
Ils bavardent sur tout ce qu'ils veulent faire.

10:30 am

At the railway station, they have to wait.
The train to the mountains is always late.

10h30

À la gare, ils doivent attendre.
Le train pour les montagnes est toujours en retard.

11:15 am

Here it comes! The bears find their seats.
They open their picnics and share some treats.

11h15

Voici le train! Les ours trouvent leurs places.
Ils ouvrent leurs paniers et partagent des gâteries.

12:00 pm

They race out of town and follow the coast.
Bear can't decide which sights he likes most.

12h00

Ils courent hors de la ville et ils suivent la côte.
L'Ours ne peut pas choisir quelle vue qu'il aime le
mieux.

1:45 pm

At long last, the journey comes to an end.
Bear has a cabin and so does his friend.

13h45

Enfin, le voyage se termine.
L'Ours a une cabane et son ami en a une aussi.

4:00 pm

The bears learn to sail on a mountain lake.
They also go climbing and they get back late.

16h00

Les ours apprennent à faire de la voile sur
un lac dans les montagnes.
Ils font aussi l'escalade et ils rentrent tard.

5:30 pm

They have lots of fun, whatever the weather.
Bear wants to stay here forever and ever!

17h30

Ils s'amusent beaucoup, n'importe quel temps.
L'Ours veut y rester pour toujours et à jamais!

What Time Is It?

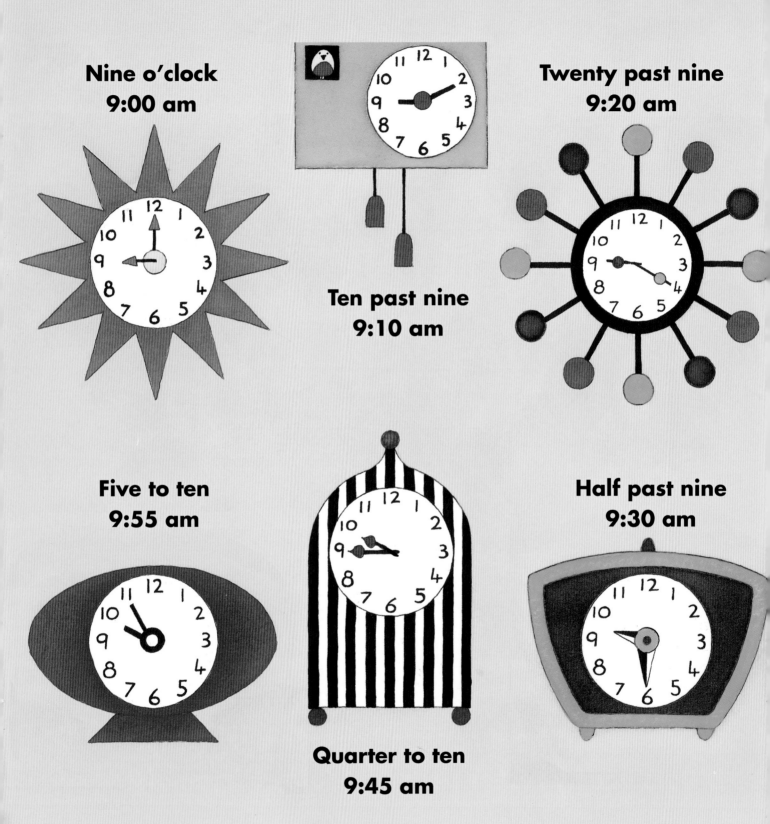

Nine o'clock
9:00 am

Ten past nine
9:10 am

Twenty past nine
9:20 am

Five to ten
9:55 am

Quarter to ten
9:45 am

Half past nine
9:30 am

Quelle heure est-il?

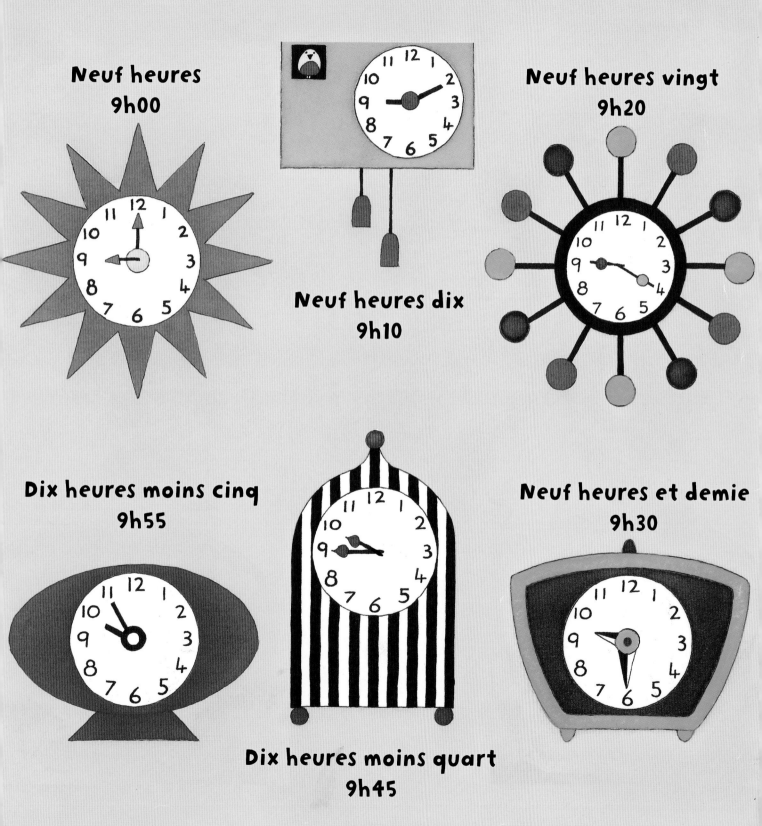

Neuf heures
9h00

Neuf heures dix
9h10

Neuf heures vingt
9h20

Dix heures moins cinq
9h55

Dix heures moins quart
9h45

Neuf heures et demie
9h30

Vocabulary / Vocabulaire

time – l'heure

morning – le matin

noon – midi

afternoon – l'après-midi

evening – le soir

midnight – minuit

second – une seconde

minute – une minute

hour – une heure

day – un jour

Barefoot Books
294 Banbury Road
Oxford, OX2 7ED

Barefoot Books
2067 Massachusetts Ave
Cambridge, MA 02140

Text copyright © 2011 by Stella Blackstone
Illustrations copyright © 2011 by Debbie Harter
The moral rights of Stella Blackstone and Debbie Harter have been asserted

First published in Great Britain by Barefoot Books, Ltd
and in the United States of America by Barefoot Books, Inc in 2011
This bilingual French edition first published in 2013
All rights reserved

Graphic design by Judy Linard, London and Louise Millar, London
Reproduction by B & P International, Hong Kong
Printed in China on 100% acid-free paper
This book was typeset in Futura and Slappy
The illustrations were prepared in paint, pen and ink, and crayon

ISBN 978-1-84686-946-4

British Cataloguing-in-Publication Data:
a catalogue record for this book is available from the British Library

Library of Congress Cataloging-in-Publication Data
is available upon request

Translated by Elizabeth Parker

1 3 5 7 9 8 6 4 2